MONICA AUGUSTINA ZHEKOV

ROS MARINUS

AND THE MAGIC BILBERRY

To the Most Curious Boy in The World, Who Inspired This Story, My Dearest Son Jordan!

Ros Marinus and the Magic Bilberry

ISBN: 9798835480883

Imprint: Independently published

Although the author made every effort to ensure the information in this book was accurate at the time of publication, the author does not assume and hereby disclaims any liability to any party for any loss, damage, or disruption caused by errors or omissions, whether such errors or omissions result from negligence, accident, or any other cause.

Edited by Ana Coman

Printed by Kindle Direct Publishing (KDP), North Charleston SC, an Amazon.com Company, USA

Once upon a time, in a little Transylvanian village within the walls of a white cottage, lived a curious little boy named Ros Marinus. His village was well hidden beyond the steep hills, covered with shiny and wild bilberry shrubs, that from afar looked like a purple blanket. A pine forest surrounded the village like a fortress wall.

The forest gave off a unique aroma, which villagers had likened to the incense used in their cosy white church.

Village life for Ros, was by no means easy. As the seasons changed through the year, he would face the challenges that came his way, helping his parents with housework and caring for their animals in the stables.

This curious and determined little boy, however had a hidden dream. A dream that made his heart race as fast as a steam engine. His secret dream was that one day his beloved, tragically blind grandmother, Ana, would be able to see again. That she would once again be able to enjoy the colours of nature. The trees, the rivers, the skies that she would gaze at for hours, watching those clouds unfurl into shapes that seemed at times, like angels dancing around the morning sun.

Early one morning, Ros rushed downstairs to eat his breakfast of milk and bread rolls, baked freshly by his mother. Afterwards, he headed off to his grandmother's house. It was a walk he always loved, wandering freely along the sandy paths, that meandered through the numerous bilberry shrubs. The bilberries were still covered by dew drops at that time of the day, making them shimmer like precious stones. Grabbing bunches of them, Ros loved to squish them between his fingers, making the juices drip and disappear into the dusty path.

Unfortunately, as much as he would have liked to have brought her some shiny fresh bilberries, he ended up arriving with only his sticky, purple palms.

Now, what was not commonly known, was that Ros believed that the bilberry's carried inside them a special kind of magic. It saddened him, that he didn't bring the miraculous fruit intact to his grand-mother Ana, because you see, Ros really wanted her to be able to see again. This was not just a child's dream, he really *believed* that this miraculous fruit had magic powers to heal the blind.

How did he know this? Ros had read this, in a mysterious old book of *Botanica*. An old book, embedded with brown floral motifs with translucent yellow pages.

His teacher 'Teofilo' had given him this book, so that he could read it during the long winter months in the mountains. This book was like no other book Ros has ever seen. Above the title "Medica Plantarum" was also written "The College of Medical Science". The pages were covered with skilful pencil drawings of various fruits and plants, along with their Latin names. Ros thought that those Latin names sounded like verses from an enchanted prayer, similar to one that his teacher Teofilo sung in the little white church.

Even more mysterious, was when he would turn the page, the drawing on the first page would overlap with the drawing on the next. These combined pictures formed new secret patterns, from which various letters could be seen if carefully observed.

That curious little boy was convinced that only he could see those letters however, as even though he showed them to his teacher Teofilo, he could not spot even one! Feeling so frustrated, Ros thought his teacher did not believe him! So determined was he, that he went on to show the pages to his mother and father, but sadly neither could see what he could see.

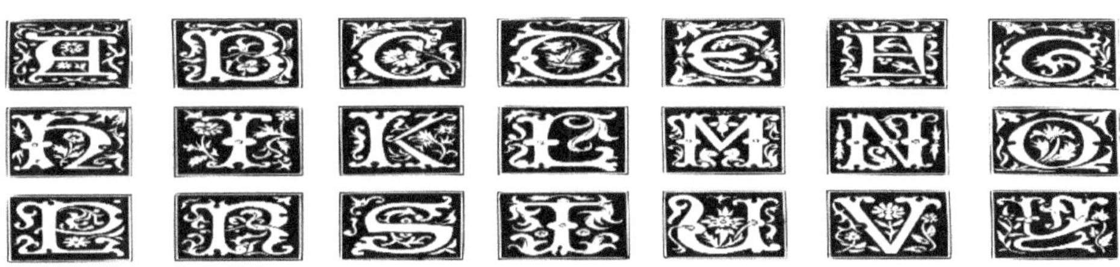

Keeping faith with his love for the book, his heart would flood with joy every time he came across a plant he found in his own village, that was described in that book.

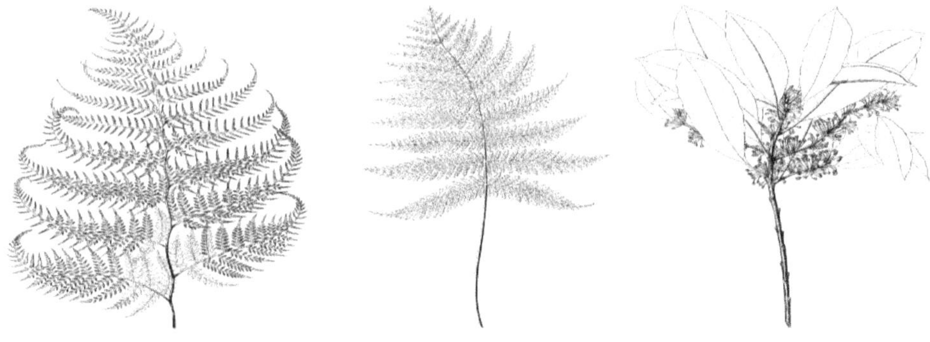

Ros would often stay awake, long into the night learning all about the plants from his magic book. Reading only by the dim light of the petrol lamp, he began to memorise all the Latin names of the plants, fruits and trees he encountered.

Staring at the ceiling in his modest dimly lit room, Ros suddenly thought about the mysterious *Atropa belladonna.* What an elegant and smooth name this deadly plant has got, he thought. His mind drifted, remembering the moment when his mother had slapped his hand. A slap he fortunately received before he could fill his mouth with that tempting black and shiny fruit, picked from the woods.

This lethal, yet enchanting plant bears the name of a beautiful lady, yet is so dangerous it can ensnare the senses, cripple the body and even take life. His face winced at the thought of this elegant and deadly plant.

In comparison however, he also learned from this ancient book, that he could freely gorge upon *Vaccinium Myrtillus*. A plant that grew wildly across his father's lands and whose fruit resembled *Atropa belladonna,* although the colour of the fruit differed slightly. "It's not fair", he thought, *Vaccinium Myrtillus* sounded much more sinister to him, than *Atropa belladonna.*
Could this magical fruit cure his grandmother's eyes?

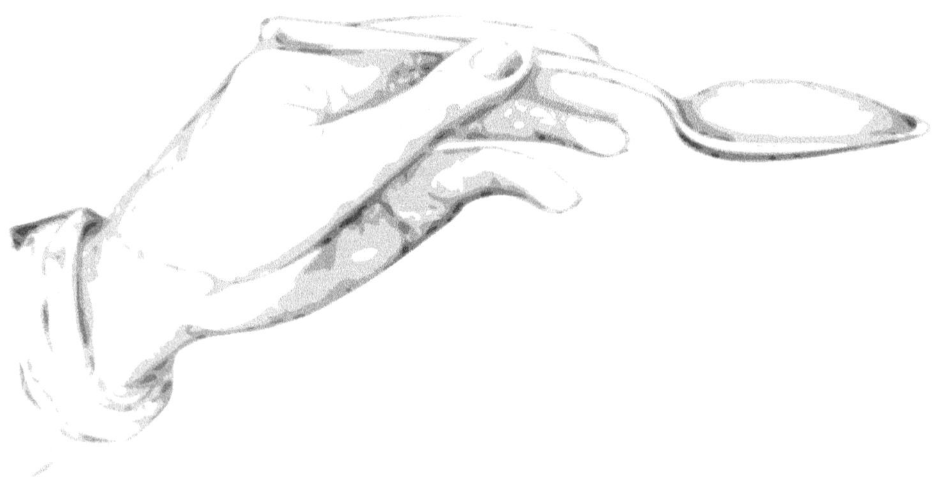

Could this even prevent people going blind? pondered Ros. We make jam from the fruit of *Vaccinium Myrtillus* not of *Atropa belladonna,* he thought. It seemed to Ros that the scientists who had named these plants, might have mistakenly attributed the wrong name to the wrong plant.

It was at that moment, right there and then, that Ros decided that when *Vaccinium Myrtillus* was going to be in season, he was going to make lots of preserves from its fruit. Ros prayed that his grandmother would get her sight back if she ate seven jars of the jam made from this miraculous fruit.

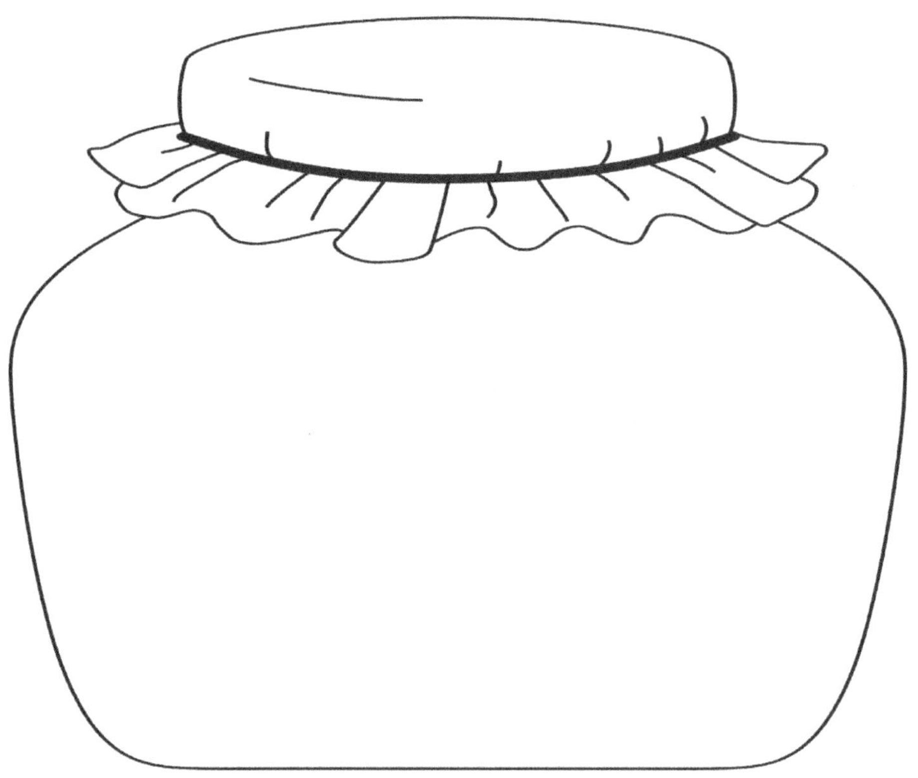

He set out into the fresh summer morning, after having contemplated throughout the night about the letter pattern he saw, miraculously appear in the bilberry drawing. As if guarded by them, the house was fronted by two tall poplar trees, protecting it like two soldiers from the story of David and Goliath. He made his way through the narrow path up to the hills, covered with the purple blanket of bilberry shrubs.

The rising sun appearing behind the forest, caressed his hair. His eyes were closed by the bright sun, that blinded him momentarily.

Protecting his face with his arm, he looked like a warrior with a shield.

"Ros Marinus, Ros Marinus" called a warm feminine voice from behind him. Surprised as he was, he slowly turned to look but there was nobody there.

"Could I be dreaming?" he thought, *"I must still be dreaming! Most of the night I was awake thinking about the letter patterns and now I am hearing voices!"*

"Ros Marinus, Ros Marinus – what is the letter that sticks in your mind?" Asked the soft voice.

At hearing this question, Ros suddenly felt a shivering cold feeling rattle his spine. *"Who could that be, how do they know?"*

"Who are you?" asked that brave little boy? He barely could move his lips to speak as the fear gripped him still.

The voice answered: *"I am the magic bilberry! The bilberry that can fulfil your wish! Just tell me the magic word from the book, that unlocks my powers and your wish will be fulfilled!"*

Ros dropped down to his knees and right in front of him saw the brightest bilberry that one can imagine. Covered in morning dew, it sparkled like a precious stone. His eyes filled with tears and his heart filled with hope.

Mesmerised, the boy uttered "Oh magic bilberry, I only remember the letter "F". I so much want for my wish to come true, but what can the magic word be? Could it be friend, flower, or even firefly? The magical bilberry responded: "For your wish to come true, the book held the clue. Close your eyes, think hard and clear, for my magic powers will soon disappear!"

"FAITH!!!!!" shouted Ros Marinus. "IT'S FAITH!"

That very moment, as he announced the magic word, the shiny bilberry disappeared and the warmth of the sun moved over his face.

Ros felt sad thinking that he might have missed his only opportunity to fulfil his dream.

Little did he know, that at that very moment, his grandmother was waking from her sleep. Although blurry at first, she could see faded shapes, colours flowed back into her life. Her room appeared before her eyes for the first time in years.

Filled with joy at the sight of Zeus, her loyal dog, she could hear the footsteps of her grandson's feet approaching quickly along the dusty path!

Like a prisoner set free, she walked through the gate and into the embracing arms of her faithful little grandson.